HOME for a TIGER, HOME for a BEAR

written by Brenda Williams

illustrated by Rosamund Fowler

Barefoot Books
Celebrating Art and Story

Spinning spider,
light and small,
Weaves a web against
the wall.

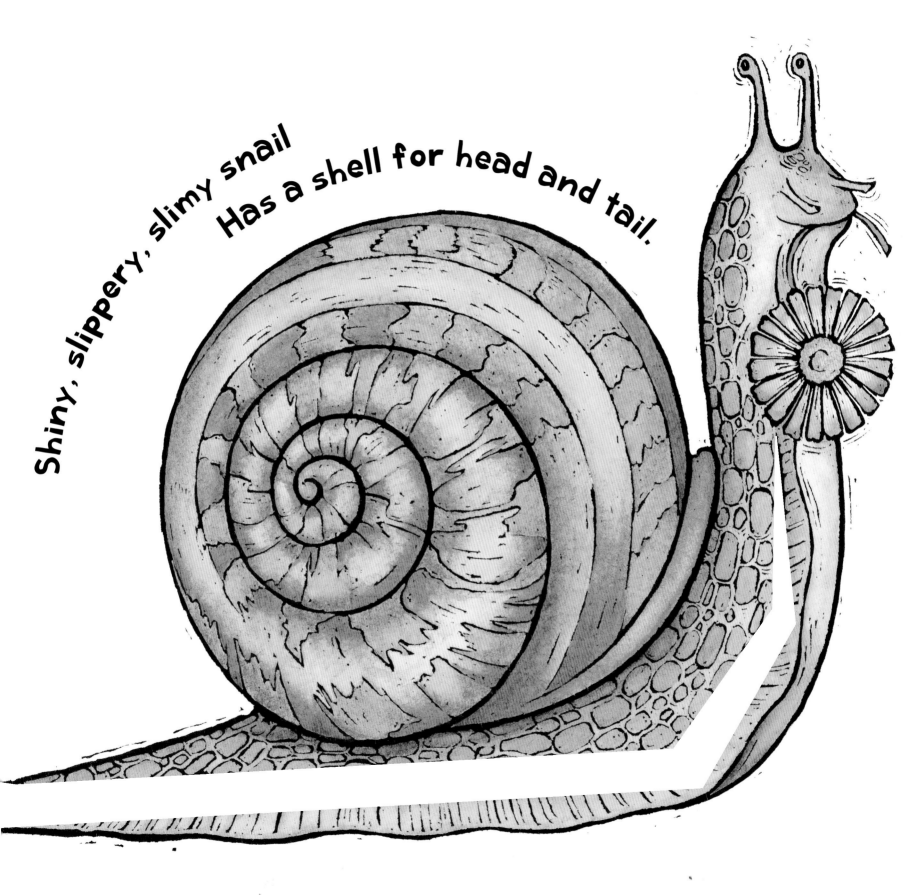

Shiny, slippery, slimy snail
Has a shell for head and tail.

Dark-eyed deer likes leafy glades;
Shyly hides in dappled shade.

Scampering squirrel, red or grey,
Makes twigs and leaves into a drey.

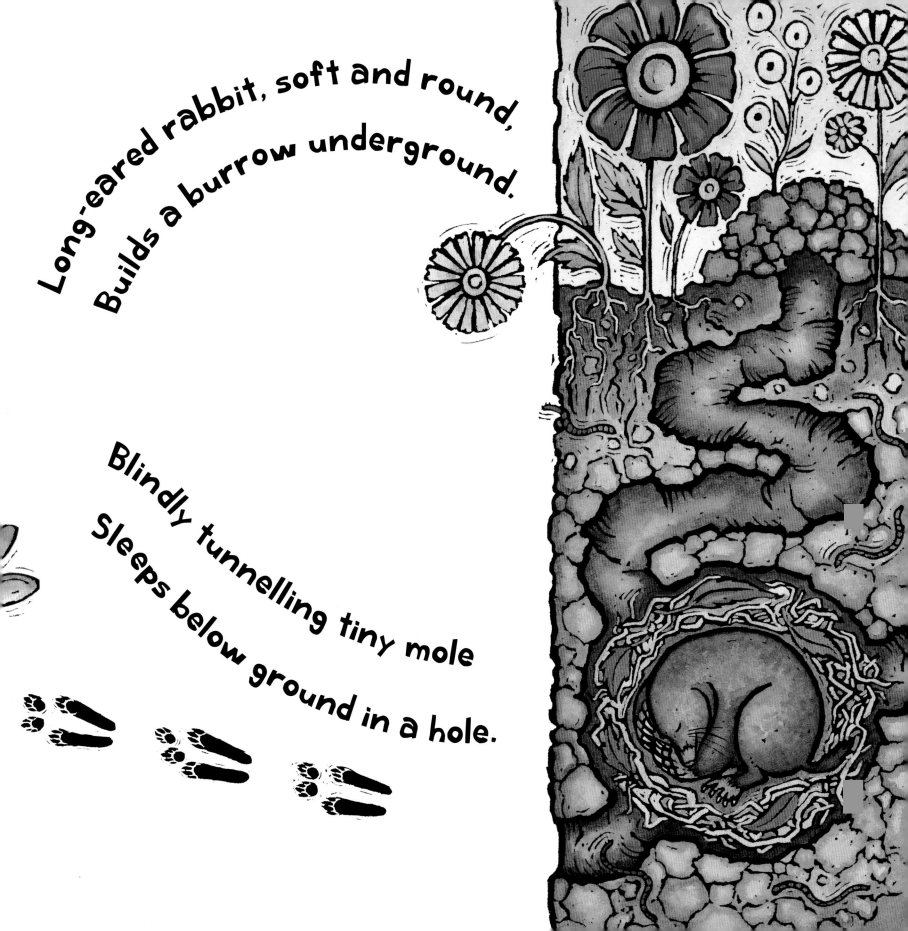

Long-eared rabbit, soft and round,
Builds a burrow underground.

Blindly tunnelling tiny mole
Sleeps below ground in a hole.

Busy beaver uses logs
To dam a stream and build a lodge.

Patient heron, with long bill,
Stands by rivers, statue-still.

Wild and fearsome, big black bear
Shelters in a mountain lair.

Soaring eagle, wings stretched wide,
Nests in eyrie on cliff side.

Lumbering elephant, ears like fans,
Rests in shade on grassy lands.

Worker termites, small but strong,
Build nests with roof-mounds all day long.

Humbacked camel, with wide feet,
Stands on sands of desert heat.

Slithering snake, with stretchy jaw,
Skulks slyly on the sandy floor.

Wallowing hippo loves a flood
And wades in rivers or in mud.

Crafty, creeping crocodile
Waits for fishes with a smile.

Leaping tiger, eyes like glass,
Likes to hide in jungle grass.

Chattering monkeys screech and yell;
Jungle living suits them well.

Kangaroo mum has a pouch,
Where baby joey likes to crouch.

Cuddly koala munches leaves;
Lives in eucalyptus trees.

Leaping frog, so green and cool
Likes to play beside a pool.

All have homes where they can rest,
But I think that my home is best!

Homes and Habitats

A habitat is a place where a plant or animal naturally lives and grows. Animals can make their homes in all sorts of places! From wet and leafy woodlands to dry and sandy deserts, every animal's home is different. Here are the habitats found in this book, along with a few of the creatures that make their homes in each:

Australian bushland is covered with lots of vegetation like scrub, which is made up of low plants and trees.

Kangaroos live in groups known as mobs, which number from about twelve to one hundred. Female kangaroos have a pouch at the front of their bodies, in which their babies (called joeys) are born.

Koalas need a habitat that includes plenty of tall eucalyptus trees. They use the trees as their home and the eucalyptus leaves as their food.

Deserts are very dry areas with limited plant and animal life. Deserts are harsh environments with very little rainfall and extreme temperatures.

Camels are well suited for living in hot, sandy deserts. They store food in their humps for long-distance travel, and their stomachs can hold more than 120 litres of water, making them valuable to nomadic peoples.

Snakes are mostly not poisonous, though a few of them are deadly. They rarely come into contact with people. They live secretively in remote areas, such as swamps, jungles, and deserts.

Gardens are plots of ground where vegetables, flowers, herbs, or fruits are grown.

Snails are often found in gardens because the soil is usually moist. They retract their heads and tails inside their shells when they sense danger, as well as during dry weather to protect their bodies from drying up.

Jungles are tangled masses of tropical vegetation, with tall trees and colourful flowers. Most animals that live in jungles can camouflage, or hide, themselves within their surroundings.

Monkeys use both their hands and feet for hanging on to branches. Some monkeys have tails that act like a third hand, helping them to hold a branch while they pick nuts and fruit.

Tigers live a solitary life in a wide range of habitats, including tropical forests, mangrove swamps, and jungles. Tigers' stripes create an excellent camouflage within thick vegetation and long grass.

Mountains are landforms that stand much higher than the land that surrounds them. Animals that make their homes here are not afraid of heights!

Black bears make dens, or lairs, under fallen trees or inside large, hollow logs. Bears can live in forests, swampy areas, or on the sides of mountains.

Eagles hunt from the air, so they are happiest in wide-open spaces, where there is little cover for their prey. They live on mountains and build their nests (called eyries) on rocky ledges, cliffs, or trees.

River habitats are often surrounded by marshland. Some animals live underwater, some animals live on the surface, and some animals live above the water.

Beavers gnaw through fallen trees to dam or block forest streams and form deep pools. They build lodges, where they live and raise their young. The lodges have underwater entrances.

Frogs are amphibians — they can live both on land and in water. They must always return to water to lay eggs, but they spend most of their time on land. During winter, frogs often live in holes in banks of mud.

Herons make nests out of sticks in bushes or trees near water. They stand very still at the water's edge, waiting for a chance to spear a fish with their long, pointed yellow bills.

Savannah habitats are made up of grasses, trees, shrubs, and drought-resistant undergrowth. Savannahs have two seasons — one hot and dry, the other cooler and wet.

African elephants mainly live in herds, south of the Sahara Desert. They have enormous ears and long, wrinkled trunks and can eat up to six hundred pounds of food a day!

Termites belong to large colonies, and each termite has its own position in the colony. The worker termites are blind, and they build underground nests that create large mounds above the ground.

Tropical-river habitats are very dense, warm, and wet. These rivers are often in rainforests, near the equator. Millions of animals are found near tropical rivers.

Crocodiles live in tropical places in many parts of the world, in or near water. They are cold-blooded and spend much of their time warming themselves in the sun on the banks of rivers.

Hippopotamuses live in grasslands in West and East Central Africa, but they spend a lot of time underwater in lakes or rivers. They come out to feed on the grassland at night.

Underground habitats are for animals that make burrows (snug holes underground) to protect them from bigger animals. Burrows also stay warm in cold weather and cool in hot weather.

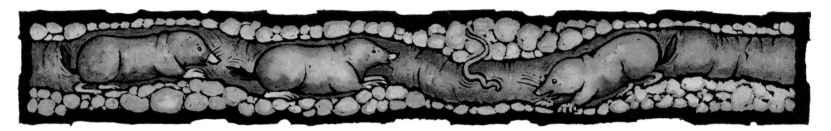

Moles like loose, moist soil, where there are plenty of worms to eat and where it's easy to dig tunnels. Moles have a very good sense of hearing and smell, but they have poor eyesight.

Rabbits have long ears, short tails, and long back legs. They burrow, or dig, underground by making holes, often under hedges. The mother rabbit makes a nest using her own fur!

Woodland habitats are large areas of land filled with trees. Animals that live in this habitat must adjust to cold winters and hot summers. They use the trees for food and as a water source.

Deer live in woodlands, especially coniferous woodlands (where pine trees grow). This is a good habitat for deer because the trees provide shelter and cover from danger.

Squirrels build nests, called dreys, in trees to sleep in at night and to raise their young. They curl up, using their tails as blankets

All about Spiders!

Did you find the spider hidden in every scene of this book? Spiders live all over the world, except in Antarctica.

Spiders spin webs as their homes and as nests for their eggs, but they also use webs to catch flies or other insects for food. Their webs are made from spider silk, which is very strong and stretchy.

Here are just a few of the many types of spiders:

Black widows use poisonous venom to kill their prey (like most spiders). While most spiders' poison is not usually strong enough to harm humans, the black widow's is an exception. Black widows live in warm places, including Africa, North America, and Southern Europe.

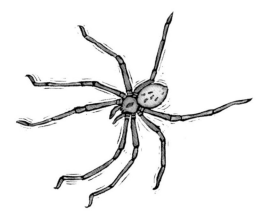

Cave-dwelling spiders live in New Zealand and Tasmania. They spin their webs from side to side to catch insects that fall from the cave roof.

Daddy longlegs make straggly webs in our homes, which they use mostly as a place to stay, rather than to catch food. We may not like them, but they do eat up many of the flies and insects that sometimes invade our homes.

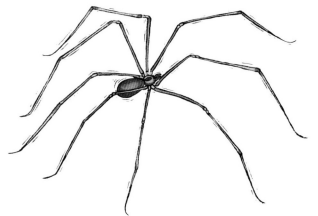

Garden spiders spin beautiful webs, which are prettiest when they are sprinkled by morning dew or light frost.

Goliath bird-eating spiders are the largest spiders in the world — about the size of a small pizza! A type of tarantula, they live in the rainforests of South America.

House spiders scurry about in our homes. They make webs in corners, attics, and sheds.

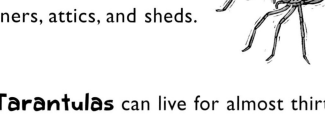

Tarantulas can live for almost thirty years! They are large and hairy and thrive in rainforests, deserts, and other warm places, mostly in South America.

Water spiders live in an unusual underwater home filled with air, called a 'diving bell'. A water spider will swim out of its bell to catch its prey on water plants, but during winter, it hibernates in its nest inside the diving bell.

For my grandchildren — Alice and Franziska for their love of poetry,
and Charlotte, Sam and Harry for the fun we have shared — B. W.

For my husband, David — love from Rosamund — R. F.

Barefoot Books
124 Walcot Street
Bath BA1 5BG

This book has been printed on 100% acid-free paper

Graphic design by Judy Linard, London
Colour separation by Bright Arts, Singapore
Printed and bound in China by Printplus Ltd

This book was typeset in 24 point Cut-out Normal and Gill Sans Regular and Bold
The illustrations were prepared in watercolour and ink

Hardback ISBN 978-1-905236-80-0

British Cataloguing-in-Publication Data:
a catalogue record for this book is available from the British Library

1 3 5 7 9 8 6 4 2

Barefoot Books
Celebrating Art and Story

At Barefoot Books, we celebrate art and story that opens
the hearts and minds of children from all walks of life, inspiring
them to read deeper, search further, and explore their own creative gifts.
Taking our inspiration from many different cultures, we focus on themes that
encourage independence of spirit, enthusiasm for learning, and sharing of
the world's diversity. Interactive, playful and beautiful, our products
combine the best of the present with the best of the past to
educate our children as the caretakers of tomorrow.

Live Barefoot!
Join us at **www**.barefootbooks.**com**